*You true
identity in
Christ!
J. Walker*

HANNAH'S HOPE

Denise M. Walker

Hannah's Hope

ISBN-13: 978-0-692-05841-1

Armor of Hope Writing and Publishing Services, LLC
Visit our Website at www.armorofhopewritingservices.com

Printed in the United States of America

Hannah's Hope

CONTENTS

Acknowledgements...............................7

Part 1

Chapter 1...10

Chapter 2..15

Chapter 3..21

Chapter 4..26

Chapter 5..31

Chapter 6..36

Chapter 7..40

Chapter 8..44

Chapter 9..49

Chapter 10..54

Chapter 11..58

Chapter 12..61

Part Two

Chapter 1......................................66

Chapter 2......................................71

Chapter 3......................................75

Chapter 4......................................78

Discussion Guide and Activities

Building Literacy...............................81

True Identity...................................84

Resources.....................................88

About the Author..............................91

Denise M. Walker

ACKNOWLEDGMENTS

I want to thank God Almighty for speaking to my heart to write this series of novels for youth. May He be glorified and magnified through my obedience!

"For I know the plans I have for you," says the
Lord. "They are plans for good and not for disaster,
to give you a future and a hope.
- Jeremiah 29:11

PART ONE:
HANNAH'S SECRET

CHAPTER ONE

Twelve-year-old Hannah Monroe sat in her seventh-period English class at Parkview Middle in Roswell, Georgia. She paced back and forth in her mind, half listening to Mrs. Westbrook. Hannah had been thinking about running away for some time. She often became anxious when the school day was about to end. Hannah had only been attending Parkview for six months. Her aunt, Loretta, had enrolled her when she had come to live with her and her husband back in July.

Hannah debated telling Mrs. Westbrook her secret but immediately decided against it. She admired her; she was her favorite teacher at Parkview. Hannah thought she was amazing. Mrs. Westbrook was older than Hannah's other teachers. She had told them that she was in her twentieth year as an educator, but she was more compassionate and able to relate to their world unlike Hannah's other teachers. Mrs. Westbrook had a tiny frame like Hannah's mother and was always well-dressed even when the other teachers would dress down. Mrs. Westbrook stood out from the rest. Her smile was inviting. Her natural hair was beautiful. It was jet black and often in an up-do with tiny black curls that seemed to tickle her cheeks.

Hannah enjoyed coming to Mrs. Westbrook's class; she felt safe around her for some reason. Mrs. Westbrook also made the subject of language arts fun. In fourth and fifth grade, her school begin to prepare them for middle school, so they had two different classes – language arts and social studies and math and science. During those years, Hannah would drag herself to Mrs. Jones' class and try to stay awake during the English block. Hannah was sure she would die of boredom and never make it to middle school. However, she survived and had finally developed a love for language arts again.

Hannah thought that Mrs. Westbrook's caring spirit was amazing in itself because some of her classmates could be extra at times, especially Monique with all that attitude. Mrs. Westbrook had to speak to her every other day about her behavior, bullying other girls, and back talking the other teachers. Monique had been in the principal's office more than Hannah could count. She had every class with her, and Hannah thought the girl was angry with the world. On a daily basis, she walked in with a stone face. For some reason, Monique wouldn't disrespect Mrs. Westbrook. Hannah just couldn't understand why she was so rude and disrespectful in the first place.

"Maybe she has a secret too and doesn't know how to tell anyone," Hannah thought to herself.

Hannah wondered if Mrs. Westbrook already knew that she had a secret. One day, she was so engrossed in her thoughts that she didn't hear Mrs. Westbrook asking her to explain the difference between similes and metaphors. Hannah was so embarrassed because everyone was looking at her as though she had sprouted two heads right before their eyes. After class, Mrs. Westbrook asked Hannah if everything was ok at home. Hannah gave her a half-smile and stated, "Sure, everything is good."

On another occasion, Mrs. Westbrook was talking

to Mr. Stewart, a seventh grade English teacher. Hannah was walking up the hall, and Mrs. Westbrook called her over to them. Mrs. Westbrook was telling Mr. Stewart that he would enjoy having Hannah in his class the following year. Mr. Stewart reached over to pat Hannah on the shoulder, and she flinched. She hadn't noticed it until Mr. Stewart apologized for startling her. Mrs. Westbrook gave Hannah another concerned look. Then Hannah quickly diverted her eyes and said, "Ok, I have to get back to connections now. I was just coming back to homeroom to grab my notebook for my technology class." She walked away telling herself, "You have to chill Hannah! People are going to find out, and you will be taken away for good."

Now Hannah was trying her best to stay focused for the final thirty minutes of Mrs. Westbrook's class. She completed her assignment quickly and raised her hand for Mrs. Westbrook to check it. The teacher came over to her desk.

"Yes, Hannah, what do you need?"

"I'm done with my comparing and contrasting paragraph." Mrs. Westbrook smiled as she read Hannah's assignment.

She then stated, "Hannah this is awesome! You are a great writer and one of my best students. Have you ever thought about becoming an author or participating in the literacy competitions that are offered each year? I remember speaking to you about this before. I love reading your writing. You should compete next year."

"No, ma'am, I haven't thought about it. I really don't think I want to, maybe in high school." Hannah stated quickly to get Mrs. Westbrook to move on to check the next student's assignment.

"You really should consider it, Hannah. I can give you some information to look over," Mrs. Westbrook continued.

"Umm, okay, maybe I'll try it," Hannah replied knowing that she wouldn't. Hannah wondered why her teachers were always praising her. Couldn't they see how hard it was for her to even pay attention in class? Hannah loved school. Everything came pretty easy to her. She loved math, but English was her favorite. Her dream was to become an author or teacher someday. She just didn't know if it would ever happen for her. However, at the moment, all she could think about was her secret. It consumed her.

"Why do people hurt others?" she thought solemnly.

About twenty minutes later, the announcements came over the intercom. Mrs. Westbrook had reached Avia's desk near the front of the room by the door. After praising Avia for a job well done, she then instructed everyone to pack up. She asked William to write the bus numbers on the whiteboard. Monet, Hannah's friend, came over to her desk.

"Hey girl, do you have any homework tonight?"

"No, I finished Mrs. Westbrook's assignment just in time, and Mr. Smith didn't give us math homework because he didn't finish teaching the lesson on integers. He promised that we would have one tomorrow though."

"Ugh, I hate math. He's always tripping," Monet stated.

"It's not that bad, Monet; I can help you. Are

you able to come over my house sometime after school?"

"I'll have to ask my mom and dad," Monet replied.

"Okay, just let me know."

Hannah was hoping her friend could come over every day after school. Maybe it would help. Perhaps then she would be safe, but Monet might also find out her secret.

CHAPTER TWO

Hannah's bus stopped at the corner of her apartment complex. She got off and turned to wave at Monet. Her friend lived in the Arborbrook Apartments a few blocks away. Hannah's heart began to race as she got closer to her front door. She took out her key hoping that today would be different.

As she walked inside, she tensed up. She could hear the television playing in the living room. Her aunt was not home from work yet, so it had to be him. Hannah walked further into the apartment, and spoke to her uncle, Malcolm, as she headed to her room. She had just recently moved in with them. She had been taken from her mom because of her drinking problem and abuse of Hannah. Her siblings were allowed to stay. Hannah wasn't sure why.

When she had lived with her mom, Hannah's mom would get drunk, scream at her, and tell her that she would never amount to anything. She would often call her a "slut" and would say that she was acting too grown around her boyfriends. Sometimes Hannah's mom would be loving and make them their favorite food and desserts. At other times, she would be drinking and threatening to kill her or beat and kick her for not hearing her instructions. Hannah just didn't get it. What had she done so wrong?

One day, Hannah's former neighbor had witnessed her mom's abuse and called the police. Hannah was so afraid. She loved her mother. She didn't want anything bad to happen to her.

"Mom just needs to stop drinking, and she will get better. Then I will be able to see her again," Hannah said to herself as she entered further into their apartment.

She really missed her mom and siblings, Malik and Brittany. Hannah would often cover her face with her pillow as she cried herself to sleep at night. She also wondered about her biological father. She wondered why she hadn't seen nor talked to him since he and her mom split up when she was five. For now, Hannah couldn't see them, and she had to try to stop thinking about it. She had written her mom a letter when she first arrived. In it, Hannah explained to her mom that she was sorry for not listening. She told her mom that she loved her and prayed for her to stop drinking. Hannah had never shown it to anyone. She had stuffed it into her book bag hoping to give it to her mom someday because she wasn't allowed to come to her aunt's apartment due to her threats towards Hannah. Her mom and aunt were sisters. The judge had ordered temporary custody to her Aunt Loretta. The other alternative was to place Hannah in foster care. She had been grateful that her aunt had chosen to take her in, or at least, at first.

Now Hannah stood and prayed softly that her uncle would leave her alone today. As she got halfway past him, he began calling her name.

"Hannah, how was school today?"

"Umm, it was ok."

"Come over here and sit next to me and tell me all about it," Hannah's uncle stated as she tried to walk swiftly passed him.

"I....I've got some work to do for class. My

teacher gave us a project. It's due Friday," she lied not knowing what else to say.

"Come over here, girl!" He persisted. Hannah couldn't understand how her aunt didn't see what was going on. Why was he still there? Her aunt and uncle often fought about him not having a job. She would pretend to be asleep some nights, and she could hear them in their bedroom arguing. She just knew they would be divorced by now, and she would be rid of the evil being that she saw daily.

Hannah hated the sight of her uncle. He had been molesting her since she moved in. It had started off great. Hannah had loved hanging out with her aunt and uncle in the beginning. They would watch movies together and hang out at the mall. She and her aunt would often have girl talk. They had often taken her shopping and out for ice cream or pizza to cheer her up.

Then, about a month later, her uncle started brushing up against her when her aunt wasn't looking. One day, he even stood in the doorway as she was coming out of the shower. Hannah couldn't believe it. She couldn't tell her aunt or this time she might go into foster care. That's what her uncle had told her the first time he touched her, and she believed it. Hannah was terrified of having to live with people that she didn't even know. Then she might never get to see her mom, dad, or siblings again. She knew she had to keep silent.

Hannah's thoughts had wondered, and she realized that she was still standing there. She had almost made it to her room.

"Didn't you hear me, girl? I said get over here."

"Why can't he just go away?" Hannah said softly before turning around.

"Excuse me, what did you say?"

"Ah….nothing."

"That's what I thought. Now bring your fine self over here."

Hannah walked over to the couch and sat down next to him. Uncle Malcolm was about six feet tall, bald head and had a graying beard. He had gained some weight since Hannah had moved in. Before, he would go jogging in the evening. Now he only sat and watched T.V. most of the time.

"You look beautiful as usual. I like that dress on you. It shows those curves," he said as he began to rub up and down her thigh.

"Stop it!" Hannah said with anger. I'm going to tell Aunt Loretta this time. I mean it!"

"And you think that she is going to believe you?" He said standing. He now towered over Hannah's small petite frame. "I'm her husband. She won't ever believe you over me," he stated with confidence.

"You know you want this. You walk around here teasing me all the time. So, I advise you to keep your mouth shut because it won't go well for you little girl."

Hannah believed his every word. She remembered trying to tell her mom about one of her boyfriends, and she wouldn't listen. Her mom had said, "Hannah, why would you say something like that. Don't you know that you could get him locked up for accusing him of that kind of stuff? Maybe you misunderstood what happened. I've been telling you about being so grown." Hannah had so many thoughts in her head.

She just wanted to understand why. Why were men so evil? Were they all like her uncle and mother's boyfriends?

Hannah's uncle began to put his hand under her dress and rub her private area and her chest. He then pulled down his pants and made her sit on his lap as usual. He didn't pull down her underwear, but Hannah still felt dirty. She began to sob as he continued to grab all over her and make her touch him as well. A few minutes later, there was a sound outside. Her uncle jumped up quickly and pushed her off of him. He zipped up his clothes and demanded her to pull down her dress. He reminded her to never say a word, or she would regret it.

Hannah hurried quickly to her room, wiping away her tears. She knew that she had to hold it all in because her aunt would ask questions. She felt all alone.

Her aunt walked through the door a few seconds later. She could hear her uncle greeting her as if he was the perfect angel. Hannah was lying down and had turned to face the wall so her aunt would think she was taking a nap and not see her tears. What could she do? When would this all end?

Hannah's mom had taught her about good touch and bad touch when she was five. She had told her that no one should touch her private areas. If they did, she was to tell her or another adult right away. Hannah's mom had given her those instructions about strangers, but she didn't know that it would be someone she knew, someone that was supposed to care for and protect her. Hannah knew that what her uncle was doing was wrong, but he kept doing it over and over again, and she was too afraid to tell.

As she lay there, Hannah began to think about her dad. She missed him. She hadn't really been allowed to see him since he and her mom had separated. Hannah and her siblings had different fathers. She often wondered why her siblings had been allowed to see their dad but not Hannah. She wasn't clear about God and prayer, but she had been trying to talk to him. She remembered being taught about it when her mom would drop them off at church, although, they hadn't been in a while.

Hannah began to pray again. She prayed for the opportunity to see or talk to her dad. She prayed for her mom to love her. She prayed for her aunt to see the truth. She prayed to tell her dad or Monet her secret, and to ask him a question, "Why did you have to leave me?"

CHAPTER THREE

The next morning at school Hannah found Monet sitting in the gym working on her science homework. They were waiting for the bell to ring for homeroom.

"Hey, Monet!" Hannah walked over smiling.

"Hey, Hannah. I'm trying to finish this science homework before the bell rings. You know I have Mr. Fisher for homeroom, and I don't need to hear his mouth about why I didn't do my homework at home."

"I know, right. Our team teachers can be strict sometimes," Hannah replied.

"Sometimes?" Monet said with sarcasm dripping from her lips while rolling her eyes for effect, a classic facial expression. They both burst into laughter. A few moments later Ashley Simmons, a girl from Hannah's homeroom and English class, walked over.

"Hey, what's up?" Ashley said to the two girls.

"Nothing." Hannah and Monet said in unison.

"So, Hannah, why don't we hang out sometime? I go to the skating rink a lot. Would you like to go with me on Saturday?" Ashley asked only looking at Hannah.

"I'm not allowed to go to the skating rink with friends yet. My parents would have to be there with us."

"What if my mom was there supervising us? Do you think they would still say no?"

"Yes!" Hannah answered looking away. Hannah hated when these kinds of things happened. She wanted to be able to do normal things. She would rather hang out with Monet instead of Ashley, but she couldn't do that either. Also, she didn't want to explain to Ashley why she lives with her aunt and uncle instead of her mom or dad. She had only told Monet, and Monet didn't even know the full story. It all felt so embarrassing to Hannah.

A few seconds later, the bell rang, and the girls headed to homeroom. Hannah and Ashley were both in Mrs. Westbrook's homeroom. Monet had gotten very quiet all of a sudden. Hannah turned to look at her as they headed up the 6th-grade hall.

"Monet, are you ok?"

"Yes, I'm good. I'll talk to you later," she responded as she walked swiftly ahead and headed into Mr. Fisher's classroom.

Hannah had a feeling that Monet didn't care much for Ashley. Ashley was one of the so-called "popular girls". Sometimes Ashley would make negative comments about other girls around them. Monet didn't like to be around those she would call "drama queens". Neither did Hannah, but she thought that Monet was a little too anti-social at times. Monet had once told Hannah that her mom didn't want her around girls that kept up mess, but Hannah thought it was more to the story. Other than Hannah, Monet didn't talk to many of the other girls on their 6th-grade team. Hannah and Monet had many things in common. They were both focused on school. They thought some of the boys were cute, but they weren't into them like the other girls. Girls like Ashley.

Monet's parents made sure she represented them well. She was well groomed and had beautiful jet black relaxed hair. Hannah and Monet were also not into name brands like some of their peers. They just liked cute girly things. They didn't have to be expensive. Still, Hannah didn't want to come across as if she were better than her classmates. She made a mental note to talk to Monet about being more friendly to Ashley. She wanted Monet to at least give her a chance.

"Please turn in your fundraiser forms." Mrs. Westbrook was saying as Hannah and Ashley walked into the room.

"Hi, ladies. How are you this morning?" Mrs. Westbrook greeted them with a smile.

"Good." Both girls stated at the same time.

"That's good to hear." Mrs. Westbrook continued.

Hannah and Ashley walked over to their seats. They sat down and continued talking about their favorite things to do until the first-period bell rang.

The bell chimed, and the girls headed to their different classes.

"Talk to you later, Ashley," Hannah stated and quickly lined up outside of Mr. Fisher's science class. She waited in line quietly as the other students talked about who liked who.

As she stood there, Terrell, one of the meanest boys on their team, bounded into her. She turned around to see what was going on behind her. Terrell looked at her with a smirk on his face and continued slap boxing with his friend, Thomas. He slapped Thomas hard on the back of the neck and ran around the corner toward the restrooms. Hannah didn't like Terrell very much. She thought he was obnoxious and goofy. Hannah had known him since elementary school, and he was constantly in trouble. Hannah rolled her eyes and turned back around in line trying to avoid an argument with Terrell. It wasn't worth wasting her words, and she was not in the mood.

Mr. Fisher finally started letting the class inside. He smiled at Hannah when she entered the room. Hannah went to her desk in the front of the classroom and took out her supplies. Mr. Fisher started calling the roll. Terrell sat right behind Hannah and began making noises. She tried sliding her desk up a little. Mr. Fisher had gotten to her name, and Terrell whispered, "You have a white girl's name."

Hannah turned around, "No, I don't. Stop acting so stupid, Terrell," Hannah stated still upset about the incident in the hall only moments ago.

"Yes, you do! And you're always trying to kiss up to these teachers. 'Hannah, you are a great student! Hannah, you're such a great writer! Hannah, why don't you try out for this?' Blah, blah, blah!' "

"Shut up Terrell! Why are you so annoying?" Hannah said with anger.

"Annoying, At least I'm not ugly! Blacky!" Terrell said loud enough for Thomas to hear. Both boys started laughing. Hannah turned back around and tried to focus on Mr. Fisher. She had never understood why some kids were so mean. She had tried her best to be nice to her classmates.

Hannah thought about Terrell's words as she sat there. Why did they bother her so much? Was it because Terrell's skin was the color of caramel and Hannah a few shades darker? Was it because his eyes were hazel? "He might be cute if he wasn't so rude and hateful," she thought to herself.

Hannah loved doing well in school and receiving positive feedback from her teachers. She just didn't know why they believed in her so much. She tried to believe too. Hannah also loved her smooth brown skin. "Am I really that dark? Am I really ugly? Forget Terrell, he doesn't know what he's talking about," Hannah continued thinking.

A few moments later Mr. Fisher called on Terrell to answer the review question that he was asking the class.

"I don't know," Terrell said under his breath and slumped down in his seat. The other students started laughing, and Hannah giggled softly. Terrell then looked at his friend and shouted, "What's funny, Thomas? You don't know the answer either."

"Alright, cut it out." Mr. Fisher told the boys.

"Hannah, help him out." Mr. Fisher continued.

Hannah looked up from her book and shrugged her shoulders. Mr. Fisher was surprised that she didn't know the answer. He then told the class the answer and called on Jared, a quiet kid, to read the next section. Terrell leaned up and whispered to Hannah, "You're still ugly! Nerd!"

Hannah then asked Mr. Fisher if she could move to a different seat. Mr. Fisher gave her a concerned look.

"Is everything ok, Hannah?"

"Yes, this desk is rocking a little."

"Go ahead." He replied.

Hannah quickly moved to the other desk. She didn't make eye-contact with Terrell the remainder of the period. She just said a prayer for the class to end soon.

CHAPTER FOUR

At the end of the day, Hannah hurried to her bus. She saw Monet talking to another girl on their team. Hannah couldn't remember her name. She sat in their normal seat. Monet climbed on a few seconds later.

"So, what's good?" Monet asked.

"I was ok today until I got to science class."

"Why? What happened in science class?" Monet sat up listening.

"Dumb Terrell!" Hannah said with frustration.

"What did he do?"

"He called me ugly and black. He said that I suck up to the teachers."

"Oh, he just likes you," Monet said laughing.

"Ewww, no! I don't like that stupid boy."

"Ok, ok, so did you hear about the new girl?"

"What about her?"

"Everyone is saying that she is thirteen."

"She does look older than the rest of us," Hannah stated.

"I know, right," Monet added.

"Oh, I forgot to tell you. My mom said that I could practice math with you next week."

"What day next week?" Hannah inquired.

"Thursday after school."

"Ok! I can't wait."

"Me either," Monet said with excitement.

"Maybe we can prank call Terrell. Remember, he gave me his phone number at the beginning of the year. I never called him of course because my parents would have killed me. But, I still have the number in my notebook."

"Girl, we are not going to prank call that fool. He probably would blame me for it even if it weren't me. And why do you think he likes me when he gave you his number."

"Because he's a player. A 6th-grade player," Monet said as they both burst into laughter.

The bus stopped, and Hannah noticed that she had reached her stop.

"Alright girl, I will see you tomorrow. Try to call me on the house phone later. You know my aunt still won't allow me to have a cell phone until seventh grade. I've asked her over and over. The answer is still 'No.' "

"Well, we will both be getting one then because my parents said I am not mature enough for one yet. I don't know what that means." Monet stated. Hannah headed down the bus steps. She waved at Monet from the sidewalk.

Hannah then entered their apartment and didn't hear her uncle. She hurried to her room and prayed that he wouldn't return before her aunt. She set her things on her bed and breathed a sigh of relief. Hannah pulled her fuzzy pink diary from the back corner of her closet. It was her favorite color. The rhinestones made it even more appealing to her. She had purchased it at the school book fair with money her aunt had given her. When asked, Hannah had only shown Aunt Loretta the small chapter book that had also caught her attention. No one knew about her diary because she wrote her deepest thoughts in it. It also contained her secret. In another notebook, Hannah created her own stories with happy endings. However, she couldn't risk someone reading the journal. She opened it up to an empty page.

Dear diary,

I miss my mom, dad, Malik, and Brittany. I wonder what they are doing right now. I wish I could call them, but Aunt Loretta said that I can't. I wonder what I did for my mom to hate me so much. Will she ever love me? She seems to love Malik and Malcolm more. I never meant to make her angry. I tried to be a good daughter. Maybe I am being too grown. Maybe that's why Uncle Malcolm won't leave me alone. It will get better soon if I can get Monet to come over more. I also want to ask my aunt about my dad. Does he even want to see me? Did he even want me? Is that why he and Mommy split up? I wonder if Aunt Loretta will let me see him.

Hannah closed her journal and quickly placed it back in her secret hiding spot. She then started working on her math homework. Math was a piece of cake to Hannah. She couldn't understand why Monet hated it so much.

After working on her math, Hannah finished her English assignment. Soon she heard someone come into the apartment. She prayed that it was Aunt Loretta.

"Hannah!" her aunt called out to her from the living room.

"Ma'am! I'm doing my homework, Aunt Loretta."

"Ok, I am going to change and start dinner. Have you seen your uncle?"

"No, ma'am, he wasn't here when I got home from school."

"Oh, he might have had some more interviews today." Hannah heard her aunt say.

She worked for about fifteen more minutes. Then she started watching some T.V.

"Hannah, Monet is on the phone."

"Ok, Auntie. I'll get it in your room. Hannah got up and went to pick up the land line. She had wondered why her aunt and uncle had one. Hannah thought everyone used cell phones, but her aunt had told her that they work during bad weather, even after their cell phones have died. Hannah guessed it made sense to have one.

"He girl," Hannah said with a smile.

"What's up?" Monet asked.

"Nothing much, getting ready to eat dinner. What's up with you?"

"Nothing much. Do you know I have an "F" in math class now?"

"An "F" Your parents are going to kill you, Monet?"

"Don't remind me, Hannah. I have got to get my grade back up. I checked my grades, and it shows that I failed the last two tests."

"I got you, girl. I can help you. You have to practice too, Monet."

"Whatever, why do I need to know that stuff anyway. I don't plan on teaching math. Ughhh......Now I'm going to be grounded. I can kiss that new outfit goodbye for now."

"Uh, you need to know how to count, crazy," Hannah said laughing. "It will come up. I'll help you," Hannah continued trying to comfort Monet.

"Did you hear that Mya and Tanaisha got into a fight in the girl's locker room during P.E. the other day?"

"No, why?" Hannah asked shaking her head.

"Girl, somebody said that Mya confronted her about Jared."

"Why are sixth-grade girls fighting over boys?" Hannah wondered out loud.

"Girl, I don't know that is why I'm glad we are not allowed to have boyfriends right now. Those boys are stupid anyway."

"Yes, they are," Hannah replied wondering if she would ever trust a boy. "Ok, Monet. I have to go. My aunt is calling me. We are having my favorite tonight. Lasagna."

"Oooh, that sounds good."

"Yes, Aunt Loretta's is the best. Talk to you tomorrow at school," Hannah continued.

'Ok, girl. Talk to you then. Bye." Monet said hanging up.

Hannah headed out of her aunt's room. As she started to step out into the hallway, she ran into her uncle. She accidentally brushed up against him.

He whispered, "I missed you today." Hannah hurried to the kitchen where her aunt was putting the finishing touches on the lasagna. It looked delicious with the layers of cheese and the garlic bread. Hannah was glad that Aunt Loretta was home and she was safe, for the moment.

CHAPTER FIVE

The school day went by like a breeze. Before she knew it, Hannah was back on the bus headed home.

"I'll be over in a little while. My mom needs me to come home first and call her. Then our neighbor, Mrs. Simmons, will drop me off at your house," Monet explained to her as they sat talking.

"Okay, see you then," Hannah said as she climbed off of the bus. She headed to her apartment and waved at one of her neighbors sitting in a chair outside. Hannah took out her key and went inside. Her uncle was standing in the kitchen. She became tense as usual. Hannah hurried down the hall to her room. She quickly locked the bedroom door. She took off her school clothes and started cleaning her room. She was excited about Monet coming over to study. She wished she would hurry.

About fifteen minutes later, her uncle knocked on her bedroom door. Hannah tried to be very still so that he would think she was asleep. He knocked again. She still didn't say anything. Then she heard him trying to open the door with something. Hannah started to tremble. "Why won't he leave me alone? He's my uncle, my aunt's husband. She really trusts this jerk?" Hannah said quietly to herself.

The next thing she knew the door opened, and he stepped into the room. He looked at her with a smile and said, "Are you trying to avoid me, sweet girl?"

Hannah didn't respond. She just wanted him to leave her room. He walked toward her with a grin on his face.

Hannah then said, "My friend, Monet is on her way here."

"Stop lying," He responded in anger.

"I'm not; she is coming to study. She just told me when I was getting off of the bus."

He didn't say anything. He just pressed himself against her and pushed her on the bed. Hannah tried to scream, but he put his hand over her mouth. He tried to unzip her pants, but she started kicking him. He then threatened that he would hurt her if she didn't stop moving. He reached his hand under her shirt and rubbed her chest. He then pulled her pants down and started rubbing her private area. She cried for him to stop. He started to unzip his pants.

Suddenly, the doorbell rang. He looked at Hannah.

"Who is that?"

"I told you that Monet was coming over," Hannah explained between sobs.

"Get up and stop crying. Fix your clothes. And you better not tell that little girl nothing," her uncle said with evil in his eyes.

Hannah hurried to fix her clothes and wipe away her tears. She went to the door. Monet gave her a strange look. Her uncle was sitting on the couch flipping the channel. The girls headed to Hannah's room. When they got inside, Hannah closed the door behind them.

"Hannah, why does it look like you have been crying?"

"No reason."

"No, stop lying. You're shaking. What is wrong? Did your uncle do something to you?" Monet said with concern for her friend.

"No, nothing is wrong. I just got in trouble for not cleaning the bathroom when I got home. What do you want to work on first?"

"I don't believe you, Hannah. I'll stay here with you until your aunt comes." Monet continued, ignoring Hannah's question.

Hannah held back her tears and smiled at her friend. They started to practice integers using the whiteboard that Hannah had in her room. The girls made a game out of it. Hannah was enjoying beating Monet at math.

After practicing math, the girls sat and talked about the goofy boys in their classes.

Monet said, "Girl, Malik is probably the goofiest, but he's so cute."

"No, he's not," Hannah said looking as if she had just eaten two bags of Sourpatch Kids.

"Why are you looking like that?" Monet asked laughing uncontrollably.

"Boys are just stupid, Monet."

"Hannah, are you sure that no one has done anything to hurt you. You can tell me. I'm your best friend."

"No, Monet. What are you talking about? Let's play Uno. That game never gets old."

Monet agreed but looked at her friend concerned.

"Oh yea, I meant to ask you. Why don't you like Ashley?"

"What are you talking about, Hannah? I'm not even thinking about that girl."

"Why do you seem to get upset when she comes

around?" Hannah inquired, not letting her friend off the hook.

"I don't do that."

"Yes, you do, Monet."

"No, I do not," Monet repeated.

"Yes, you do, so tell me why?"

Monet looked at Hannah and continued to focus on her Uno cards. They played for another five minutes before Monet spoke.

"Hannah, a girl in my fourth-grade class bullied me. She was just like Ashley. Everybody thought she was so cool! I thought she was just mean."

"How did she bully you, Monet," Hannah asked with concern.

"She would push me when the teacher wasn't looking, and take things off of my desk. She would try to scare me in the bathroom with her other popular friends. I believe she was older than the rest of us. She was way taller. I think she had been held back twice."

"I'm sorry that happened to you, but Ashley is not like that."

"She could be. You don't really know her. That's why I only talk to you. I want to stay away from drama."

"I feel you, girl! But try to give Ashley a chance."

"I can try, but if she starts some mess, I'm done," Monet said to her friend.

The girls put away the Uno cards and started practicing some more math problems before Monet had to leave.

"Hannah, you know I haven't forgotten about what I asked you?"

"Monet, nothing happened. My uncle was upset about me not doing my chores. That's all."

"Okay, Hannah! You know I'm here for you."

Hannah didn't respond to her friend. She knew she couldn't tell anyone her secret, even her best friend. She was still excited to have Monet there with her. She was glad she was safe.

CHAPTER SIX

A few weeks had passed, and Hannah had only had one encounter with her uncle. She thought that maybe he was feeling guilty about what he had been doing or was afraid that Monet knew the truth. He tried to be nice to her, but she tried her best to avoid him like the plague.

Hannah got off of the bus and headed to her apartment as usual. She got excited when she didn't hear the T.V. in the living room. Hannah then remembered her uncle telling her aunt that he had a few more job interviews lined up that day. He was not at home. Hannah was home alone again and didn't have to fear.

A few moments later, the phone rang. She walked quickly into her aunt's bedroom to grab it. To Hannah's surprise, it was her dad. She would never forget his voice. Hannah smiled and was nervous at the same time.

"Hannah, is that you? How are you?"

"Umm, I'm fine."

"Is your aunt there? I am trying to reach her. She called me a few days ago. She must have gotten my number from my brother."

"No, she is not home from work yet."

"Oh, Okay." her dad replied slowly.

"Dad, how are you?" Hannah asked.

"I'm good Hannah. I really miss you. That is why I'm trying to contact your aunt. I'm glad she reached out to me. She left a message that you have been asking about me."

Hannah's eyes brightened. She was quiet for a few moments. She blinked back tears.

"Hannah, are you still there?"

"Yes, Daddy, I'm here. I miss you, too."

"Is everything okay over there? Your aunt also told your Uncle Joseph about having custody of you now," he continued.

"Yes, it's ok. I'm in the sixth grade now."

"I know, you are growing up so fast. How are your grades?"

"They're good. I love to write," Hannah said.

"That's good to hear. Listen, I know that your mom and I didn't communicate well, but I want you to know that I have been trying to see you. Your mom wouldn't allow me to see you. Then your aunt called me. I was thankful to get her message. Write down my cell number for your aunt and you as well. Make sure you put it in a safe place."

"I won't lose it. I promise."

"Now, if you need me or just want to talk, call me."

"Yes, Daddy!" Hannah replied with the brightest smile.

Hannah wrote the number down twice, once on the notepad on the counter and then in her math notebook.

"Hannah, I have to get back to work now, but remember to call me sometime, and tell your aunt she can try me back on my cell. I'm at work most of the time; I'll try to answer. I live with your Uncle Joseph, my brother, and his wife, Aunt Melissa."

"Okay! Daddy. Oh, Ah, Daddy."

"Yes, Hannah?"

"I really miss you a lot."

"I miss you too, sweetheart." Mr. Monroe replied before hanging up. Hannah headed to her room with tears in her eyes. This time they weren't because she was sad but because she had finally heard her dad's voice.

She picked up the cordless phone again and called Monet. Monet answered the phone after the third ring.

"Hi, Hannah. What's up?"

"Monet, guess what?"

"What?"

"I just spoke to my dad."

"That's cool! I know that you said you hadn't seen or heard from him."

"Yes, he said that he has been trying to see me. He also gave me his phone number."

"That's cool, girl! I'm really happy for you."

"Yes, it is! I wrote his number down in my math book, and I will try to call him soon."

"I'm glad to hear that you heard from him. Did you tell him about your uncle?" Monet asked.

"What do you mean?" Hannah pretended to be confused again.

"You know what I mean, Hannah. You're my friend, and I don't want bad things to keep happening to you. I know what I saw the other day."

"WHAT ARE YOU TALKING ABOUT, MONET?" Hannah began to panic.

"Calm down, Hannah. See, if it was nothing, you would not be that afraid. You have to tell someone."

"I told you that I got in trouble for not cleaning the bathroom."

"Okay, whatever Hannah. I will be praying for you. I really think I should tell my mom."

"There is nothing to tell your mom. My Uncle is cool, Monet."

"Okay, Hannah."

"Monet, I've got to go do my chores, so I don't get yelled at again." Hannah said, trying to sound convincing.

"Okay, whatever you say. I'll see you tomorrow. Love you, girl!" Monet said with sadness.

"Love you, too," Hannah replied before hanging up and collapsing into a river of tears. She couldn't hold it in anymore. She was tired of faking it.

CHAPTER SEVEN

After enduring her uncle's abuse the next day, Hannah just wanted to run away. He had pulled up her skirt and made her sit on his lap again. He acted as if he owned her. He continued to rub all over her, making her lie next to him on the sofa. He soon became tired of her whimpering and sent her to her room. Hannah then climbed into her closet and stayed there until her aunt came home. Aunt Loretta arrived about an hour and a half later. She seemed tired and started yelling at Hannah for not taking out the trash. Hannah ran to the kitchen to take the garbage to the backyard. Her aunt noticed that her eyes were puffy.

"What's wrong, Hannah? Why does it look like you have been crying?"

"No reason, I'm just not feeling good."

"Are you sure? I didn't mean to yell at you. I just had a long day. What is going on?"

"My stomach is bothering me." Hannah lied.

"Oh, go and get some Tylenol off of my dresser, and go make you a cup of tea with milk in it. You will feel better soon."

"Okay," Hannah said softly.

After dinner, Hannah went to her room and pulled her diary out of her secret hiding place in the closet. She lay across the bed and started writing.

Dear diary,

I'm so excited. I was able to talk to my dad today. It has been many years since I've seen him. He wants to see me. I'm so so so excited! I thought that he didn't love me. I hope Aunt

Loretta will let me see him. I also pray that Monet doesn't tell anyone my secret. Uncle Malcolm may really hurt me then. I don't want to be taken away from Aunt Loretta or my friend or even my dad. Why can't she just see how evil he is? He pretends that he is so innocent. I just want him to go away. I may have to run away if they find out. I can't go into foster care. I also can't take his hands all over me anymore. What am I going to do?

Hannah closed her journal again and put it away. Then she pulled out her other notebook. She began creating another story with a happy ending. Hannah loved reading stories with happy endings in school too. They made her believe that her life would get better someday. She wrote for about thirty minutes and then pulled out her math book to do some practice problems for the quiz the next day. Hannah sat and stared at her dad's phone number that she had written on the inside cover. She wanted to tell him her secret. Somehow, she knew that he would believe her. She sat and wondered what he was doing at that moment.

Hannah lay there trying to remember the last time her mom and dad were together. She remembered her father tossing her in the air and catching her when she was about four. She smiled at the memory. "Why would my mom keep him from me," Hannah whispered to herself. "What did he do so bad? What did I do so bad? Why were Malik and Brittany's dad able to see them? Did she hate him that much?" Hannah continued. She started to cry again as she thought about how mean her mother was to her at times.

Hannah then recalled one of the many times she didn't hear her mother calling her from the living room because she was listening to music. That was her way of zoning out. The music would help her to relax.

That day, she had finally gotten up to see what her mom wanted after Malik came into the room to tell her. Her mom then began to curse at her. She tried explaining that she had headphones on her ears, but her mother told her to shut up. Hannah then asked her what she needed her to do. Her mom then hurled a brush at her. She had been using it on Brittany's hair. Hannah had ducked out of the way. She stood near the bathroom door not knowing what else to do. Her mom had finally said, "Just get out of my face, Hannah! You are no help. You're just like your sorry daddy."

Hannah had headed back to her room and sat on the side of the bed. She continued to wonder if her mom had ever loved her.

The phone's ringing brought her back to the present. She could hear her aunt talking to someone. Hannah realized her aunt was talking to her dad. She started to smile again.

"How are you, Richard?" Aunt Loretta said into the receiver. She couldn't hear the entire conversation.

A few minutes later, Hannah heard her aunt calling her from her bedroom. She went to the door and opened it.

"Yes, Auntie!"

"Why didn't you tell me your daddy called here yesterday?"

"Oh, I forgot," Hannah replied.

"He wants to spend some time with you. How do you feel about that?"

"I would like to see him."

"Okay, do you have any studying to do on Saturday? I was going to let you spend the day with your dad while your uncle and I go see a movie or something."

"No, I don't have any work to do," Hannah said trying to hold back her excitement.

"Okay." Her aunt replied as she was still speaking to Hannah's dad on the phone. Hannah's aunt then said, "Your dad needs you to be ready by 10:00 on Saturday. He'll be here at that time to pick you up."

"Okay, Auntie," Hannah responded as she stepped back to close the bedroom door. She danced with excitement.

As Hannah headed outside, she saw her uncle pulling into the parking lot. She instantly became angry. Her uncle got out of the driver's side. He waved as she walked down the sidewalk. She waved back without smiling.

Hannah just wanted to be a sixth grader and hang out with her friends. She didn't want to be touched anymore. Hannah just wanted to be normal and feel loved. Being able to see her dad was definitely a good start.

CHAPTER EIGHT

Saturday had finally arrived, and Hannah had changed at least ten times. She wanted to look her best for her dad. She hadn't seen him for quite some time. Hannah was even a little nervous. She wanted to look like his "little princess" as he used to call her. As Hannah was finishing her bun in her hair and adding a little lip gloss, she heard the doorbell ring. Aunt Loretta answered it. Hannah could hear that it was her dad. Her aunt told him to have a seat. Hannah yelled from her bedroom

"Hi, Daddy! I'm almost ready."

"No problem, take your time," Mr. Monroe responded.

Hannah could hear him talking to her uncle. He was asking him how things were going. Hannah was shocked again to witness her uncle speaking as if he were a model citizen. "How is it that NO ONE can see it?" Hannah thought to herself.

She finally came out wearing her long sleeve, brown Calvin Klein top with the matching boots and her navy Levi's. Hannah made sure her shirt covered her bottom, and she had stretched it, so it didn't cling to her. Her natural hair was in a bun with the curly bang hanging down in her face. She had her coat with the fur around the collar because it had been freezing lately in Georgia. Hannah hugged her aunt and said goodbye to her uncle before heading out the door to her dad's car.

Mr. Monroe drove an older modeled blue Nissan

Altima with a dent in the bumper. Hannah wondered how he had damaged his car as she climbed into the front seat. Her dad got in on the driver's side and headed out of the parking lot. She stared at her dad for a moment. He was still her hero. He looked the same: medium height, low haircut, and still handsome. Hannah thought she looked like him. They both had that beautiful brown skin. "How can I be ugly?" she said quietly to herself.

"Where to?" Hannah's dad asked smiling.

"Can we get a burger, some fries, and a large shake?"

"Oh wow, that sounds like lots of calories."

"Daddy!" Hannah said holding up her hands pretending to pray.

"Okay, but I'll have to say no to the shake and fries. I'll just have a burger. The doctor says that I have to watch what I am eating."

"Oh, yea! Why?"

"We'll talk about it later. Let's enjoy this day."

Hannah looked at her dad and smiled. She was remembering when she was younger. Her dad would play hide and seek with her. She remembered searching for him. He tried to hide behind the couch, but she could see his shoes sticking out. She was still daddy's girl.

Mr. Monroe turned off the highway into a strip-mall. He pulled up to JJ's Grill. It had awesome food. Her classmates talked about it all the time. Hannah had eaten there with her aunt a few times on girls' day out. She always enjoyed their talks.

Hannah and her dad got out of the car and went

inside. He chose a booth near the back. Hannah couldn't contain her excitement.

"Have you eaten here before?" Mr. Monroe asked.

"Yes, with Aunt Loretta. I love their food!"

"I do too."

The waitress walked over with menus and asked them if they were ready to order. Mr. Monroe said, "Give us a few minutes."

The waitress added, "Do you know what you would like to drink?"

Hannah quickly said, "Yes! I would like a cookies and cream milkshake." Her dad smiled and shook his head.

"I'll take an unsweet tea, please." Mr. Monroe added.

"Okay, coming right out," the waitress stated and headed to take the next order.

"Unsweet tea! Gross," Hannah stated dramatically.

"It's better for you than so many sugars," her dad replied.

"Why are the healthy things so nasty?" Hannah said with a grin.

"I'm not sure. Wait until you get older, you'll understand."

Hannah and her dad sat and talked about when she was younger as they waited to order their food. Soon the waitress returned with their drinks.

"Have you decided what you would like to eat?" the waitress persisted.

"Yes," Mr. Monroe replied.

"Finally, I'm starving," Hannah stated. They both placed their orders and continued talking.

"I really missed you, sweetheart." Hannah's dad

told her.

"I missed you too. Daddy, can I ask you something?"

"Yes," he replied.

"Why did you and Mommy separate?"

"Wow," he said as he searched for the right words to say.

"Well, baby girl, it just wasn't working out."

"Why wouldn't she let you see me? What did you do so wrong?"

"I don't know, Hannah. Your mom loves you. Don't ever forget that."

"I believe that she does, but sometimes she was so mean to me, mostly when she was drinking. I miss her, Malik and Brittany though."

"I know you do, but you have to live with Aunt Loretta and Uncle Malcolm now. I wish you could come with me, but I don't want to hurt your aunt. She has been really great, allowing me to see you after everything with your mother. That has to be hard not allowing her own sister to see her daughter. And plus, I live with my brother and his wife. I can't afford my own place right now."

"Dad, can I please come and live with you? I can sleep on the couch."

"Hannah, I know you are missing us, and this is hard for you, but I don't have my own place. I would love to have you with me. It's hard right now. Maybe your aunt will allow you to spend a few weekends with me. I know that she is taking good care of you." Hannah's dad stated trying to comfort her. Hannah looked away for a moment.

"Hannah, your aunt is taking good care of you, right?"

"Umm, yes, of course, Daddy!"

"Good, we'll talk to her about spending more time when we get back."

"Okay," Hannah said with a hint of sadness. She loved her aunt, but she would have never thought that her uncle would hurt her. Her dad hadn't noticed because he was asking about the hold up of their food.

The waitress finally came with their burgers. Hannah's mouth was watering, ready to dig in. She smiled at her dad and continued their conversation. She had become very good at hiding her secret.

"So, where are we going after this?" Hannah inquired.

"Where would you like to go? We have the whole day to ourselves."

"Can we go over to the mall and then the arcade?"

"Sounds good. Let's eat and then we will be on our way."

As they ate, Hannah thought to herself, "Maybe there is hope for me after all. As long as I'm not alone with Uncle Malcolm, I'm safe."

CHAPTER NINE

Hannah walked into the gym Monday morning. She was all smiles. Hannah couldn't wait to tell Monet about her weekend. She had an amazing time with her dad and became depressed when he had brought her back home.

Hannah walked over to Monet and greeted her as usual. Monet responded slowly.

"I thought you were upset with me," Monet said.

"No, I'm good. What's going on?" Hannah asked her best friend.

"Not much just ready for the bell to ring. I hate coming in here. There is always some girl drama. Your little friend, Ashley almost got into it with a seventh grader about some boy name Miles."

"Miles? Who is that?" Hannah inquired.

"I'm not sure, but that girl said that Ashley better watch herself and stop trying to talk to her man. I told you! You don't really know her," Monet continued dramatically.

"Really?" Hannah asked.

"Yes, girl, really," Monet echoed grabbing her book bag and heading to homeroom.

As they walked, Hannah said, "Oh, I hung out with my dad on Saturday. We had a really good time."

"That's cool, girl. How is he doing?" Monet asked.

"He's doing great. I would like to spend more time with him. We both asked my aunt if it was okay for me to spend some weekends with him. She said that she didn't mind."

"That's good; you should spend more time with your dad. You said you hadn't seen him in a long time. You never said why he left. You also never really told me why you had to come and live with your aunt and uncle."

"Hannah said, "It's a long story."

"Monet replied, "We are best friends, Hannah. You can tell me anything even about ----"

Monet noticed Hannah's expression change. She didn't want to upset her friend again.

"Never mind, see you in class. Talk to you later," Monet said.

"Don't forget about lunch," Hannah added.

"Yea, that too. Alright, girl!"

Homeroom went by quickly, and Hannah was headed to Mr. Fisher's science class. She prayed that Terrell was absent; she didn't feel like dealing with him. As Hannah headed down the hall, she heard Terrell coming out of Mr. Smith's room. Hannah sighed loudly. Terrell walked up to Hannah and said, "What's up, Blacky?"

Hannah walked away ignoring him. He got behind her as they headed into the classroom. She walked up to her desk and sat her notebook on top. Terrell pushed it on the floor. Hannah turned around.

"Pick up my notebook, Terrell!"

"I didn't knock it down, so I'm not picking it up," Terrell said laughing.

"You did knock it off of the desk," Hannah said steaming.

"I said I didn't, and I'm not picking up your stupid notebook."

"You get on my nerves! Why won't you grow up?" Hannah added. She didn't want Terrell to ruin her good mood, so she kneeled down to pick up her notebook. As Hannah reached for her notebook, Terrell bumped her, and she fell. The whole class started to roar with laughter. Hannah was so angry; she stood up and slapped Terrell leaving a red mark on his face.

Mr. Fisher had just entered the room from the hallway and noticed that Thomas and Jamal were trying to hold Terrell back.

"What is going on in here?" Mr. Fisher demanded.

"I was getting ready to sit down, and Terrell knocked my notebook on the floor. I asked him to pick it up, and he said no. Then I bent down to grab it, and he bumped me, and I fell over." Hannah explained.

"And you slapped me, Blacky," Terrell said with anger.

"Did you slap him, Hannah?" Mr. Fisher asked with surprise.

"Yes, I did after he pushed me down."

"I didn't push you down," Terrell said lying.

"Yes, you did!" Hannah repeated.

"Okay, let's just have Mr. Wright speak to both of you. Terrell, you have got to start being more serious about school. It's never your fault, but you're always in the middle of something," Mr. Fisher stated fuming.

Hannah couldn't believe that she had gotten so upset and slapped Terrell. Now she was headed to the assistant principal's office. What if he called her aunt? She would be in big trouble.

They walked into Mr. Wright's office and sat down in the waiting area. They were instructed to sit on separate ends of the room. Mr. Wright was on the phone. He sounded like he was already talking to someone's mom. Hannah was so embarrassed; she had never gotten sent to the principal's office.

A few moments later, Mr. Wright called them into his office. He shook his head when he saw Terrell.

"Again! How many times has this been, Terrell?" Mr. Wright asked already knowing the answer.

"I don't know. I didn't do nothing. Ya'll just always think it's me. She slapped me." Terrell stated trying to sound convincing.

"You really think I believe that! Really?" Mr. Wright said with a slight smile.

"You don't have to believe it. That's what happened. Look at my face! It's red, dude."

"And you had no part in it at all," Mr. Wright continued.

"She thought that I knocked her notebook down, but I didn't. I might have done it by accident."

"Accident, okay. Well, if you come to my office again, you are going home for a few days. And it won't be an accident! DO I make myself clear?"

"Yea, man, I guess."

"You heard me, Terrell. Now go back to class and learn something. Here is your pass."

"Okay," Terrell replied still pretending to be the innocent victim.

After Terrell left, Mr. Wright talked to Hannah about keeping her hands to herself and letting an adult know. He told Hannah that he was shocked and had only heard good things about her. He then sent her back to class and instructed her to stay away from Terrell and to let him know if there were any other issues. Hannah was relieved. She didn't want to lose her temper like that again.

The rest of the day went smoothly. Hannah was thankful that she only had one class with Terrell. She walked out of Mrs. Westbrook's class and headed to the bus. Monet was talking to Mrs. Westbrook about her grade on the figurative language test. Hannah couldn't wait to tell Monet everything. She was only able to tell her a little bit before class started. After her day at school, Hannah was not looking forward to dealing with her uncle. She prayed he was not at home as she boarded the bus.

CHAPTER TEN

Hannah got off the bus and waved goodbye to Monet. She then headed up to her apartment. When she entered, she started to get excited. There was no sign of Uncle Malcolm. Hannah hurried to her room and changed out of her school clothes. She then walked into the kitchen to start her chores. As she was cleaning the kitchen, Hannah picked up the phone to call her dad but heard the front door open. She quickly hung up and started putting away the dishes. Her uncle walked passed her but didn't say anything at first. He placed something in the trashcan and went back into the living room. He flipped on the T.V. to Law and Order. He loved watching that show. Hannah started washing the last few dishes in the sink and swept the floor. After cleaning the kitchen, she vacuumed her bedroom and headed to clean the bathroom. When Hannah opened the bathroom door, Hannah rolled her eyes. She hated this part of her chores. The toilet was the most disgusting of all. She lifted the toilet seat, "So gross!" she said covering her nose.

As she was cleaning, she heard her uncle coming down the hall. She froze. He peeked into the bathroom.

"Oh, I'll go use our bathroom in the bedroom. Also, don't forget to put the clothes in the washing machine before your aunt comes home."

"Okay, I will," Hannah replied nervously.

Her uncle headed into his room. Hannah started

to breathe more easily. A few minutes later, she heard their room door shut and heard him walking back into the living room. She was now cleaning the tub and running the shower.

Hannah didn't hear Uncle Malcolm come into the bathroom. He then stepped closer to the tub and smiled. She looked at him with fear. She prayed that he would turn around and head back into the living room. Hannah turned back around to continue cleaning the tub. He came up behind her and told her to stand up. She continued cleaning. He then yelled, and Hannah rose quickly. He pushed her against the wall and began to grab her chest area. He then started to kiss her. She turned her head to the right and then the left to avoid his alcoholic breath. He grabbed her face and kissed her roughly as he reached for her private area and squeezed causing Hannah to wince at the pain. She started to cry. He was hurting her, and he didn't seem to care.

"Why won't you just leave me alone?" Hannah whispered between her tears. He kept kissing and touching all over her. Then suddenly, as if a switched was turned off, he stopped and walked out of the bathroom. Hannah moved quickly to close the door and locked it. She slid to the floor and cried like she never had before.

Hannah heard the front door to the apartment close. She waited a few minutes until she knew it was safe. She came out of the bathroom and went to the kitchen to call Monet. Monet didn't answer so Hannah hung up. A few minutes later, the phone rang. Hannah grabbed it.

"He-llo," Hannah said shivering.

"Hannah, what's up?" Monet said with concern in her voice.

"Hannah. Hannah, say something." Monet stated.

"Yes," Hannah said through her tears.

"What happened? What's going on? Monet asked.

"He hurt me again, Monet."

"Who, your uncle?"

"Yes, he's gone now."

"Hannah, hang up with me and call your dad. You have to tell him."

"But, I'm afraid. My uncle said that no one will believe me. What will my aunt say? Will she hate me?"

"Hannah, I'm putting my mom on now," Monet said.

"N.." Hannah was saying, but it was too late. Mrs. Williams had the phone.

"Hannah, sweetheart. Monet told me what she witnessed. Is your uncle doing anything inappropriate to you?"

Hannah didn't speak. Mrs. Williams waited and then said,

"Hannah, you can tell me."

"But, I'm afraid, Mrs. Williams. My aunt... She will really hate me. Promise that you won't tell anyone."

"I can't promise that, Hannah."

"But….what will happen to me?

"Sweety, you have to tell. I tell you what, I'll give you a few days to talk to your aunt, and I'll ask her if you can come over with Monet to study while she is at work."

"No, I can't," Hannah continued to sob.

"If you are afraid to tell her, what about talking to your father?" Monet's mom continued.

"I can't, Mrs. Williams."

"Yes, you can, sweetheart. It's going to be okay."

"Are you sure?"

"I can say that you will be safe again."

"Okay. I'm going to tell him."

"Okay, sweety, If you don't I will talk to your aunt.

"Monet and I are going to come over and get you until your aunt makes it home.

"He's not here right now."

"Yea, but he may come back. We are on the way."

"Okay, I'm scared."

"It's going to be okay, Hannah."

CHAPTER ELEVEN

Hannah had been enjoying the weekends with her dad. That was one of the positives in her life at the moment. They would hang out at the mall together. They went out to different restaurants, and even to the movies at times. It was never a dull moment even if they were just talking about him growing up.

A few days after Hannah had confessed her secret to Mrs. Williams and Monet, she asked her aunt about seeing her mom and siblings. That evening, Aunt Loretta tried to contact her mom to set up a time for Hannah to visit, but it didn't go well. When she called, Hannah's mom seemed very angry. Hannah could hear her on the other end of the phone.

"Loretta, why are you calling me? You took my child away from me!" Hannah's mom stated with rage.

"Tamika, you know that is not true. You have to stop drinking, sis. Your daughter needs you. Why are you so mean to Hannah anyway?"

"I'm not mean to that girl. She's going to do what I tell her. She's getting too grown. Did you talk to her sorry daddy? I'm sure you did, trying to make me out to be the bad person."

"Yes, I did talk to him, and no, I did not make you out to be a bad person. He has been taking her on the weekends."

"Why are you letting him take her? He didn't want to see her before. That's my child. Well, whatever!"

"Tamika, you know that is not true. He has tried

to see Hannah. Remember, I was over there a few times when he called you trying to see her." Aunt Loretta quickly reminded her.

"As I said, whatever, Loretta!" Hannah's mom yelled before disconnecting the line. Aunt Loretta then turned to Hannah and told her to give it more time. Hannah agreed with sadness in her eyes but continued to pray that she would come around.

After the call that evening, Aunt Loretta told Hannah that she needed to run out for about an hour. Hannah didn't know what to say. Uncle Malcolm was at home too. She knew what that meant. She still hadn't told her dad about the abuse. Mrs. Williams had told her she would give her a few days. Things had gotten better since she was now going over to Monet's after school. Aunt Loretta thought it was because they had been working on a project and that Hannah was still helping Monet with her math.

She did not want to stay there with her uncle. She thought about asking to go back to Monet's until her aunt returned, but she had just been over there earlier. Hannah didn't know what else to do, so she looked at her and said, "Okay."

As soon as Aunt Loretta left, Uncle Malcolm began to violate her again. Hannah fought back as best she could. He almost raped her this time, but her size gave her an advantage. She was able to get away by slipping through his grip and moving as fast as she could to the front door. She ran out of the apartment and down the stairs. She walked around outside praying for her nerves to relax. About thirty minutes later, her aunt pulled up. She looked at Hannah with a questioning stare. Hannah quickly thought of a lie. "Aunt Loretta, I just wanted to get some fresh air. It feels good out here." After that, her aunt didn't ask any questions. It seemed that Hannah's explanation was good enough.

CHAPTER TWELVE

That night Hannah could hardly sleep. She made sure her room door was locked. She had been up for hours, trying to fall asleep. It was challenging. Fear gripped her. Each time she thought she heard a sound, she jumped up.

The following day she finally got up enough courage to tell her father. She was terrified, but she remembered what her dad had told her on one of their outings, "If you need anything, call me."

Hannah headed to the bus stop. Monet had told her that she would be a few minutes late, so she wasn't on the bus. When Hannah arrived at school, she headed to homeroom. She asked Ashley if she could use her cell phone. The girl didn't respond at first. Then she seemed to notice the sadness in Hannah's eyes. Ashley then asked with concern, "Girl, are you okay?" Hannah lied, "Yes, I just need to tell my dad something right away. I forgot to tell him before I left." Hannah explained. She still hadn't told Ashley about living with her Aunt and Uncle. Ashley gave her the phone, and Hannah stuck it into her pocket and asked the teacher to go to the restroom. She prayed no one was in there.

Hannah walked quickly down the hall and waited for the one girl to come out. She then stepped inside and dialed her dad's cell; she had memorized the number. The phone rang two times before he picked up. She was nervous wondering what her dad would say.

"Hi, Hannah. What's up?"
Hannah was quiet for a moment. Her dad spoke again,

"Hannah, are you there."

"Yes, Daddy I'm here."

"What's up?"

"Umm…I've got to tell you something."

"What's going on?"

"Daddy, you have to promise not to get angry."

"What? Why am I going to get angry? What is going on, Hannah?" Mr. Monroe said sounding concerned.

"Do you promise not to tell?"

"Tell what? What are you talking about?"

"Daddy, ummm….Uncle Malcolm." Hannah started saying.

"What about your Uncle Malcolm, Hannah?"

"Umm…he has been…ummm….touching me."

"What do you mean; he's been touching you?"

"He's been umm…touching me in my private area. He has thrown me down on the bed and tried taking off my clothes. Daddy, he hurts me. He does this a lot."

"WHAT?" Mr. Monroe said trying to hold back his fury.

"Daddy, are you angry with me?"

"No…of course not. I'm angry with him."

"Daddy, you can't tell anyone. Aunt Loretta will be upset with me. Uncle Malcolm said she won't believe me."

"Hannah, listen to me carefully. Are you at school now?"

"Yes."

"I need you to go to a counselor and tell them what you just told me. I am coming up there. Do you understand me?"

"But..but? Daddy, I'm scared," Hannah said starting to cry.

"Hannah, there is nothing to be scared of. Do what I said, and I'll be there as soon as I can. No one else will hurt you."

"Okay, Daddy," Hannah said with fear in her voice.

"It's going to be okay, princess," her dad assured her before hanging up.

Hannah walked quickly back to class and handed Ashley her phone. She then walked over to ask Mrs. Westbrook if she could get a pass to see the counselor.

Hannah's heart was racing, but she knew what she had to do. Mrs. Westbrook looked at Hannah anxiously.

"Are you ok, sweety?"

"Yes, Ma'am," Hannah responded with sadness.

"Hannah, if you need anything, anything at all, let me know, okay."

"Yes, Ma'am," Hannah said quietly. Mrs. Westbrook, with a loving expression, squeezed Hannah's hand and spoke with her eyes. Hannah quickly pulled her hand away and blinked back tears.

She stepped outside of the classroom, headed down the hall and opened the door to the counselor's office. She told Mrs. Reid that she really needed to talk to her.

"Sure, sweetheart. Come on in and have a seat."

Hannah suddenly started shaking. She knew that

her dad had promised that everything would be fine. Hannah wasn't sure. Mrs. Reid came from around her desk.

"What's going on?"

"Umm, my dad told me to tell you…" Hannah began.

"Tell me what?" Mrs. Reid asked.

"He told me to tell you my secret."

"What secret, sweetie? Is something going on?" Hannah shifted in her seat and reluctantly started talking.

PART TWO:
HANNAH MOVES IN WITH HER DAD

CHAPTER ONE

Hannah had recently been removed from her home again. She was removed this time from her aunt and uncle after reporting her abuse to the school guidance counselor. Her uncle, Malcolm, had seemed like the most caring individual at first. He would smile and seem so concerned about Hannah in front of everyone else, but she knew the truth.

After reporting her abuse, Hannah felt relieved. She almost ran out of the office when the counselor picked up the phone to report it. Mrs. Reid had tried to comfort Hannah, but it felt like her heart would explode. By the time Hannah arrived home, social services were there talking to her aunt. Aunt Loretta had looked shocked. The social worker was explaining that Hannah was being removed. Now she was beginning a new school year with her dad.

Hannah continued to reflect as she got closer to her new school.

Although Hannah missed her mom, her aunt, and her siblings, she truly enjoyed being with her father and being a normal kid. She had only been with him for two months, but she was so excited. He was very loving and encouraging. However, she did not like them not having their own place. Her dad had explained to her that he could not afford to live on his own, and his brother had offered for him to live with them.

"Oh well, I will just have to get used to it. I'm

safe with Daddy now, and I don't want to leave him."
Hannah said as she turned the corner a block from
her house.

She was headed to Redan Middle School. She
was beginning a new journey there as a 7th-grade
student. Hannah still lived in Georgia, just further
away from Roswell and Uncle Malcolm.

As Hannah continued walking to school, she
started to reflect on her very short thirteen years. She
had just turned thirteen on June 8. Hannah had been
trying to understand why her life was so messed up.
"Why do I have to go through so much pain? Why
can't I be with both of my parents? Maybe my mom
is doing better now, and I can see her. Were my
classmates experiencing the same things and just not
talking about them?" Hannah asked herself.

She turned on to Cedar Avenue. Her uncle's
house was just a couple of blocks away from the
school. She wondered what this new middle school
would be like. Would she make friends? Would she be
able to trust anyone? Hannah had always tried to
work hard to do her best in school. She was going to
miss her friends and teachers, especially Mrs.
Westbrook. She was in a new school now. She knew
that she had to do her best. She wanted to make her
dad proud.

As she entered the building, Hannah became
more and more uneasy. She thought about how some
students from her old school would joke or make
comments about her name being a white girl's name.
There was one person she surely wouldn't miss,

Terrell. "Kids like that are just ill-mannered," Hannah's grandmother would always say, at least that's what Aunt Loretta had told her. Hannah smiled. "Sounds like Grandma Liz had so much wisdom," Hannah thought. Grandma Liz was Hannah's mother and Aunt Loretta's mom. She passed away from liver cancer when Hannah was an infant. She wished she could have gotten to know her. She loved looking through the phot albums with her mom and aunt and hearing the stories about her.

Hannah had always ignored the comments about her name. Now she finally knew the meaning of her name. It was a name from the Bible. Hannah had been taught about the existence of God and Him as the creator. She also remembered her mom telling her that Grandma Liz had named her. Her mom told her that her grandma loved God and loved attending church. Hannah had often wondered why they never really continued going to church after her death. Hannah's mom would sometimes drop them off at church when she was a few years younger. She remembered what they had taught in children's church, and Hannah looked up the meaning of her name online. She found out that her name meant grace and favor. She didn't really understand what those two words meant either, so she looked them up too. She learned that grace meant forgiveness and mercy or to show kindness. Favor kinda meant getting special treatment. She liked both words. That made her cherish her name even more!

Hannah's thoughts were interrupted when she heard two other girls talking behind her as she headed to the cafeteria. It was now 8:15 a.m. and the area would soon be buzzing with her new peers sharing their summer adventures and possible similar nightmares. Hannah walked up to the serving line and greeted the cafeteria manager. Her badge read "Ms. Noami." Hannah was trying to decide on pancakes or toast and cereal. She grabbed the toast, cereal, and a vanilla milk carton.

When she got up to the register, Ms. Noami asked,

"How are you, sweetie?" Are you new here at Redan? I haven't seen you before."

Hannah replied, "Yes ma'am. I am starting my seventh-grade year here."

"Oh, ok! Well, you try to have a great year. Now go on and make some new friends," Ms. Noami said with excitement.

"Thanks!" Hannah responded softly and headed over to an available seat. Hannah sat down at an empty table. She had decided as her summer vacation was ending that she would keep to herself. She wanted to start off fresh. She already had so much on her shoulders.

Before she could protest, a guy walked over to her table with a scowl on his face. He was tall, about Hannah's complexion and appeared to be athletic.

"Good morning," Hannah said trying to sound friendly.

"Good morning," he said in a sarcastic tone.

"I'm Hannah. What's your name?"

"Uh, Keith Jackson, why?"

"Ahh, I was just asking since you sat at the table with me. I was trying to be friendly. That's all."

"Umm," Keith said stuffing food in his mouth as he continued eating his breakfast. Hannah still couldn't understand why some people were so rude. He immediately reminded her of Terrell.

Hannah got up a few minutes later, said goodbye to Keith and dumped her tray. She headed to the school gym where she was told to wait in the mornings. This reminded her of her previous school.

As she entered, there were students all over in their fresh new gear. Hannah's dad was only able to purchase her a few new things to start off the year. She went to sit down next to another female student reading a novel. The student looked up, greeted Hannah, and became engrossed again in her reading. Hannah looked around wondering who the seventh-graders were. She sat and hoped for a great year.

CHAPTER TWO

The bell rang, and Hannah headed to homeroom. She had already received her schedule when she attended Open House with her dad. When she got to her hallway, she was greeted by a very friendly girl.

"What's UP, I am Brittany Hines, what is your name?"

"Uhh, I'm Hannah Monroe," she replied nervously.

"Welcome to Redan Middle! Who do you have for homeroom?" Brittany continued.

"My schedule says, Mr. Kelly."

"Oh, that's what's up. That's also my homeroom. I'm headed there now."

Both girls entered Mr. Kelly's room. They both smiled with great anticipation. Brittany invited her to sit in the seat next to her.

Brittany didn't waste any time, "So, where are you from? I don't remember seeing you last year, were you on the other sixth-grade team?"

Hannah thought to herself, "Dang, she is nosy! Breathe already!"

"I live nearby. I attended Parkview Middle last year. Then I moved, so now I ……..................."

A few minutes after Britanny and Hannah sat down, in walked Keith Jackson. Hannah stopped mid-sentence. Brittany was asking Hannah a question when she noticed her staring at Keith.

Brittany asked curiously, "Dang girl, you move fast! Have a crush already, huh?"

Hannah looked at her puzzled, "Wait, what?"

Brittany laughed and said, "You heard me, Ms. Thang!"

Hannah brought Brittany up to speed of what had transpired at breakfast.

Britany responded, "Don't pay Keith no attention, he is always like that. I think he was having some issues at home last year. At least that was the rumor."

"But this is the first day of school, dang," Hannah said.

"I know, girl. Some of these people stay angry."

Keith found a seat in the back of the classroom by himself. He then glanced up at Hannah. Their eyes met for a moment, but Keith quickly turned away. Hannah wanted to go over and talk to him, but she decided against it. "I know how it feels to go through something and not have anyone to talk to about it," Hannah thought with sadness. She continued talking with Brittany for a little while longer.

At about 8:55 a.m., Mr. Kelly started calling the roll. Most of the students seemed to know each other. Hannah started to feel out of place. The bell rang at 9:00 a.m. and they all settled down. Mr. Kelly came to the front of the room and began passing out agendas and other paperwork for their parents to sign. Hannah hated this about the first day of school. She was not excited about going through rules and expectations. Each year was about the same.

"Keep hands, feet, and all objects to yourself. Don't get out of your seat without permission. Don't bully, and on, and on."

Mr. Kelly seemed like a cool teacher. He was also on Hannah's schedule as her math teacher. She prayed to continue making good grades. She enjoyed English language arts because reading had helped her to take her mind off of her abuse while living with her mother and aunt. She would get lost in the character's world. She had often prayed for her own happy ending. It finally seemed to be coming true.

Hannah and her classmates continued listening to Mr. Kelly for the next hour, which seemed like an eternity. He finally said, "Ok, ladies and gentlemen, we are going to do a getting to know you activity. I will give you a slip of paper, and you will write down three things about yourself. It could be where you were born, how many siblings you have, your family, hobbies, or favorite subject. Then you will walk around the room and find someone that you have something in common with and introduce each other." Hannah started to feel nervous again. She didn't want to share things about her family. She reluctantly completed the assignment. She then walked around to find a partner. Hannah walked up to Keith who was still seated.

"Keith, can I see what you have?" she said. He didn't answer. He just pushed the paper towards her. She noticed that he didn't have any siblings. Right now she was the only child at her dad's house. He also enjoyed reading.

"Well, Keith, it looks like we are partners. We both love to read."

"Oh, great! I was hoping that no one had the same thing as me."

"Keith, do you mind me asking you a question?"

Hannah asked gently.

"You already did," he replied with frustration. "Go ahead; I don't have to answer."

"I was just wondering why you seem so angry or upset and it's only the first day of school?"

"What's your name again?" Keith asked.

"I'm Hannah, Hannah Monroe."

"Well, Hannah, you won't understand even if I explained it to you."

"I might." Hannah continued.

"Let's just get this introduction thing over with," Keith stated with rising frustration.

"Okay, no problem.

As Hannah introduced Keith, there were a few chuckles around the room. Some of the guys were whispering about Keith's hobby, reading. Hannah hated that some of her peers liked to be critical of the smallest things. She was already exhausted, and she had to make it through the remainder of this boring day.

CHAPTER THREE

Hannah finally arrived home. She headed inside to try to take a nap before dinner. She greeted her aunt, Melissa, her dad's brother's wife.

"How was your first day?" her aunt asked.

"It was ok, Auntie!" Hannah replied as she headed to her bedroom.

"That's all you have to say?" Aunt Melissa inquired.

"Yes, I met some new people. The teachers were nice, but they always are on the first day. I'm just a little tired that's all."

Hannah walked into her bedroom. It wasn't really hers. She lay on the bed and tried to rest. She couldn't wait for her dad to make it home. He worked as a maintenance man for a local hotel. Hannah loved how her dad took pride in his job, and everyone loved him. He didn't make a lot of money, but things could have been worse.

The first few days of school were always exhausting. Every class goes over the agenda and some of the same procedures from the previous year. Before taking a nap, Hannah grabbed her diary.

Dear diary,

I finally got away from Uncle Malcolm. Will he come after me? I do miss Aunt Loretta. I wonder what she is up to. I love living here with Daddy though. He is such a good daddy. He works a lot, but when he gets off, we get to hang out. He always tells me that I am smart and that I'm his princess. I feel safe now. I can take a nap without being afraid that someone will

come into my room. I can walk into the house without my heart racing. Aunt Melissa and Uncle Joseph are cool.
I do get nervous around boys. Maybe I can talk to Daddy about that.

She closed her diary and drifted off to sleep. When she woke up an hour later, she walked past the living room and went into the kitchen to make a sandwich. She then headed back to her room. Hannah was glad that she didn't have any homework. She texted her new friend, Brittany, to see what she was up to. Hannah's dad had purchased her a cheap cell phone a few weeks after she came to live with him. He told her that he wanted to be able to reach her.

Brittany lived a few blocks away. After texting back and forth for a few minutes, Hannah grabbed the new book she had checked out and started to read. She really missed talking to her best friend, Monet.

A little while later, Hannah told her aunt that she was going outside for a few minutes.

"Ok, don't go too far. You are not familiar with this area yet. I need to know where you are."

Yes, Ma'am." Hannah replied.

No one her age was outside. Hannah actually enjoyed it. She didn't walk very far because things were so dangerous now, and she knew what her aunt had just told her. She stopped at the park just up the street from her house. There were some guys playing basketball and a few small kids on the swings. Hannah sat on the bench near the swings. She took out her phone and scrolled through her new social media pages. She then heard male voices. Hannah looked up and noticed that Keith and another one of his friends were walking in her direction. She began to panic, "Oh no, why is he in this area. Does he live around here?" Keith and the other guy walked up. She also recognized Keith's friend. He was in her social studies class. Hannah awkwardly said, "Hi." She wasn't sure if they could hear the crack in her voice.

CHAPTER FOUR

"Do you live around here?" Keith asked before Hannah could ask the same question.

"Yes, I do," Hannah replied.

"I've never seen you around here before." Keith's friend stated.

"I just recently moved over this way."

"Oh, ok."

"Well, we were just hanging out. Are you enjoying Redan so far?" Keith asked.

"Kinda," Hannah replied wondering why Keith had been so impolite earlier.

"Oh, yea, and sorry about my attitude earlier today. I was having a bad first day. I wasn't ready to come back."

"Oh…" Hannah said.

"Well, see you around at school," Keith said as they headed in the opposite direction. Hannah was glad because her hands had started to sweat.

A few moments later, she picked up her cell phone to call her friend, Monet.

"Hey, Monet."

"Hannah, how are you? Girl, I miss hanging out with you."

"Me too, girl! What's been going on since I left?"

"Well, Mrs. Westbrook asked about you after you had to leave all of a sudden just before the end of the school year. And she moved up to seventh grade with us."

"I miss her."

"She misses you too. We all miss you, even Terrell asked about you."

"Terrell does not miss me, Monet. If so, then why was he so mean to me?"

"I don't know. He's matured a little bit though. How are you liking your new school and being a seventh grader?" Monet asked her best friend.

"It's ok! I will just have to get used to it. I really love being with my dad. He doesn't have his own place. He lives with his brother and his wife, but it's better than being there with Uncle Malcolm. And seventh grade is about the same as sixth."

"That's true Hannah. I am glad that you are away from your uncle. We never know what someone is going through, even as kids."

"Yea, I miss Auntie Loretta though," Hannah said sadly. "I wonder if she is upset with me?"

"Girl, I'm sure she misses you too. Has your dad said anything about any of them?"

"No, he only told me that I am not allowed back there because Uncle Malcolm is still over there. He seemed angry about that. And he told me to keep praying for my mom to come around."

"Well, you are safe now. Maybe I can talk my mom into letting me come visit or you visit over this way. She could take us to the mall or the arcade."

"I would love for us to hang out at the mall out here, go get pizza, ice cream or something. Thanks again for being my friend, Monet. Tell Mrs. Williams thank you, too."

"I will," Monet said before hanging up.

Hannah got up and headed home. She no longer had to be afraid. She could now be a kid and feel safe. She now knew that there was hope for her. She knew that she would be okay and no longer had to endure secret abuse. At least this part of her story had a happy ending.

Discussion Guide
"Building Literacy"

1. According to the novel, why was Hannah so afraid to tell about Uncle Malcolm?

2. How would you describe him using a list of adjectives?

3. Do you think that Hannah could have done anything different to stop the abuse? Why or why not?

4. Do you suspect that one of your classmates is being abused? Why?

5. Now that you have read about those who assisted Hannah, how could you help a classmate that might be going through abuse?

6. Have you ever experienced such abuse? If so, be sure to inform an adult that you trust right away. Remember that it is not your fault.

7. Do you think that things would have been different for Hannah if her dad would have been allowed to see her sooner? Why or why not?

8. Do you know a student like Terrell? Why do you think individuals like him are so mean to their peers?

9. How did Monet display true friendship to Hannah? How can you be a true friend to others?

10. Do you think Hannah will have a close friend like Monet at her new school?

11. Do you think something is going on with Keith Jackson? Explain.

12. Hannah often hid her true feelings from others but wrote in her diary. How do you think this helped her?

13. Which part of Hannah's story would you change? Why?

"True Identity"
Questions and Activities

The Bible never promises that we wouldn't endure pain in this world, but God does tell us that He will be with us through those ordeals. Below are a few scriptures for you to understand more about Him.

1. *"For I know the plans I have for you," says the Lord. "They are plans for good and not for disaster, to give you a future and a hope," (Jeremiah 29:11 - NLT).*

This is a well-known scripture. It is one of God's many promises to us. How do you think it relates to Hannah's struggle? What do you think God's good plan is for Hannah? What do you think God's good plan is for you?

2. *"Children are a gift from the Lord; they are a reward from him," (Psalm 127:3 - NLT).*

The above scripture helps us to understand that God loves those that experience horrible things like Hannah. Children are all a gift from God even though evil things may happen. Never give up. Make a list of adjectives that describe Hannah as God's gift. Then make a list that describes you as God's gift.

3. *"People who conceal their sins will not prosper, but if they confess and turn from them, they will receive mercy," (Proverbs 28:13 - NLT).*

This scripture tells us that individuals like Uncle Malcolm have to repent for hurting others. If not, they won't prosper. If they do, God will have mercy on them. God has the power to change their hearts. We have to pray for them. God loves them too. Ask God to help you pray for people like Uncle Malcolm.

4.   *"But if you refuse to forgive others, your Father will not forgive your sins," (Matthew 6:15 NLT).*

Although Hannah endured lots of pain at the hands of Uncle Malcolm, God still desires that she forgive him. Why does the scripture say we need to forgive? Do you think this would be difficult for Hannah? Why or why not? Do you think this would be difficult for you? Why or why not?

5.   Christ already knows that it is hard for us to let go of such pain and forgive. That is why He gives us the strength to do so. If you don't have a relationship with Christ, pray to Him, repent of any sins, and surrender your life to Him today. He can see you through anything. Things may still happen in our lives, but He can lead and guide us through it all. We just have to trust Him. Through Him, we are made whole again.

6.   Hannah had often prayed about her situation, but she didn't quite understand everything about God. What are some things you don't understand about God? His Word (the Bible) tells us all we need to know about Him. Find at least three scriptures that tell you more about Christ. Explain the meaning of each in three different paragraphs. Give each one a title.

7.   What are some other ways Hannah or we can grow closer to Christ?

8.   *"Thank you for making me so wonderfully complex! Your workmanship is marvelous—how well I know it,"*

(Psalm 139:14 NLT).

Have you ever questioned yourself after someone said something negative about you? Why?

This scripture tells us that we are the workmanship of God. We were designed wonderfully by Him. Those are the only words we should focus on, not the negative words of others. How could this scripture have helped Hannah when she was dealing with Terrell? How can it help you in school when dealing with bullies? Be specific.

9.   Extension activity – On a poster board, design a social media page that identifies the overall theme of Hannah's Hope. Add some scriptures that relate.

10.   Extension activity – Research signs of child abuse. Take notes. Then create a brochure that could assist someone in identifying the signs. Share it.

RESOURCES

1. School counselors, teachers, and another trusted adult should be informed about someone abusing you, a friend, or classmate.

2. National Center for Missing and Exploited Children – (1-800-843-5678)

3. National Hotline for Crime Victims 1-855-4-VICTIM (1-855-484-2846)

4. National Child Abuse Hotline (1-800-422-4453)

5. Doors of Hope 4 Teens and Young Adults http://www.doorofhope4teens.org/ The hope line: (803-570-2061)

6. After Silence – (1-800-656-HOPE) www.aftersilence.org

7. Focus on the Family Counseling Consultation Line – (1-855-771-HELP) (4357)

Hannah's Hope

"GOD IS OUR REFUGE AND STRENGTH, ALWAYS READY TO HELP IN TIMES OF TROUBLE." (PSALM 46:1-NLT)

ABOUT THE AUTHOR

DENISE M. WALKER is a wife, mother, middle school educator, author, and mentor. She is a Christian blogger and the host of Hope in Christ w/Denise and Building Literacy and True Identity podcasts. She loves hanging out with her family. Denise also enjoys writing, editing, coaching and promoting Christian and children's literature through her business and book club ministry. She lives in Georgia with her husband and their teenage son.

Denise M. Walker

96694404R00052

Made in the USA
Columbia, SC
04 June 2018